TELEPHONE
TAG

YEARLING BOOKS are designed especially to entertain and enlighten young people. Patricia Reilly Giff, consultant to this series, received her bachelor's degree from Marymount College and a master's degree in history from St. John's University. She holds a Professional Diploma in Reading and a Doctorate of Humane Letters from Hofstra University. She was a teacher and reading consultant for many years, and is the author of numerous books for young readers.

For a complete listing of all Yearling titles, write to Dell Readers Service, P.O. Box 1045, South Holland, IL 60473.

TELEPHONE TAG

SHERRY SHAHAN

A YEARLING BOOK

Published by
Bantam Doubleday Dell Books for Young Readers
a division of
Bantam Doubleday Dell Publishing Group, Inc.
1540 Broadway
New York, New York 10036

ISBN 0-440-41304-4

Printed in the United States of America
June 1996
10 9 8 7 6 5 4 3 2 1

35184457

For kids with braces,
birthmarks, pimples and frizzy hair

CHAPTER

1

Heather shut the refrigerator door when she heard the telephone. She glanced at the kitchen counter—where the cordless phone was —but the receiver was missing. What else was new? Her stupid brother never put anything back when he was done.

The phone rang a second and third time. "Don't hang up!" she screamed while she hurried down the hall. "I'm coming!"

Heather barged into her brother's bedroom. The smell of stinky sweat socks made her eyes water. She pinched her nose. The phone rang more loudly as she closed in on the unmade bed. Broken potato chips and a half-eaten slice of pepperoni pizza littered the striped sheets.

They had two phones and two phone lines. The kitchen phone—a cordless—was for the residence, and the business phone was in Dad's bedroom. Each one was connected to an answering machine. Heather had memorized their different rings.

Ring. Ring. Ring.

"This call better be important," she mumbled, "since I risked my life to come into this room."

Heather lifted the edge of the comforter with the tips of her fingers. Gross! There were probably all kinds of creepy crawlies hiding underneath: potato bugs nibbling ruffled chips.

No phone.

"It must be under the bed."

Heather dropped to her knees. And, sure enough, there it was, wedged between a pair of soccer cleats and a can of styling mousse.

She switched the button to Speak and stood up. "Hello?"

There was silence; then a voice said, "Do you have pigs' feet?"

Sometimes the cordless phone had static. "Huh?" she asked.

"Better put your shoes on so no one will notice."

"Is this a crank call?" As soon as she said it, she knew she was right, and switched the button to Off. She weaved back across the cluttered carpet and shut the door behind her—to keep the rest of the apartment from getting contaminated.

The caller was probably one of Todd's friends, she decided. Guys in the eighth grade didn't have all their brains. Everyone knew that. Even TV doctors stated that females matured faster than males. This was proof. She'd stopped telling riddles when she was in kindergarten. Now she was in the sixth grade—that was almost six years ago!

She'd never even made a crank call. Well . . . except for last summer when most of her friends were on vacation. And there wasn't much to do. But no one had answered the phone so it didn't count.

Heather tromped into the kitchen. The refrigerator shelves were crowded with platters left from her dad's dinner party two nights ago: crab-stuffed mushrooms, black bean torte, hearts-of-palm quiche. Her dad owned Cahoots Catering Company, a two-person operation that made fancy food for wedding receptions and bar mitzvahs.

Heather popped the plate of meatballs into the microwave, then searched for the toothpicks with curly plastic tops.

The phone rang at the same time as the oven beeped. Heather jumped. No way! Crank callers never called back. That would be like a criminal returning to the scene of the crime. It was probably her best friend, Jamal. She'd be back from her ballet lesson by now.

"Hi, Jamal," Heather said into the phone. "How was class?"

The voice was fuzzy with static, but it was male. "If you don't like the pigs' feet riddle, I have another one."

"Don't you know it's against the law to make

crank calls?" Suddenly Heather remembered the detective show on TV the night before. "I telephoned the police right after you called. A couple of undercover officers are on their way over to set up a trace." Then she added, "Are you a friend of my brother's?"

"The only reason I called back—" he started.

Heather hung up before he completed his sentence. *Why should I care why he called back?*

Heather took the plate of meatballs out of the oven. She went to the phone and punched in Jamal's number. "Guess what?" she said when Jamal answered. Then she blurted the details of the last half hour. *"Do you have pigs' feet?* Have you ever heard of anything so lame?"

"Who do you think it was?"

Heather shrugged and gobbled another meatball. "I didn't recognize the voice. But maybe that's because we had a lousy connection. Sometimes the cordless phone picks up static." She paused, sighing. "I thought riddles went out with acid-washed jeans."

"Don't be so sure."

Heather stopped chewing. "What do you mean?"

"I think it was someone from our class." Jamal spoke in a whisper, as if this was top-secret stuff. "Someone who likes you, but doesn't know how to tell you. You know how guys are. At school they act like we have some dreaded disease. Then they call about homework and are halfway cool." She paused, giggling. "I think you have a secret admirer."

"I should've known you'd find something romantic about this." When Jamal grew up she'd probably write romance novels or be a soap opera star. She had the perfect complexion to be an actress. It was as soft and smooth as melted chocolate.

"I think it was Brian Benson," Jamal said.

"What? The most popular guy in the entire sixth grade?" Heather tried to smooth her thin bangs over the pink birthmark on her forehead. It was shaped like an artichoke. And slightly larger than a quarter. "The only time he even talks to me is to borrow notebook paper."

6

"See what I mean?" Jamal sounded excited. "He's never borrowed paper from me. Not even a pencil or eraser."

"If it is him it's even worse. I told him I called the police. Then I hung up on him—two times!"

Jamal tried to reassure her. "Hey, you didn't know it was him. So none of that counts. Believe me, I know about these things. Haven't I watched every episode of *The Young and the Dissatisfied* for a year? Every show is about relationships, right? I'm almost an expert on the subject."

Heather thought for a minute. "Yeah, but—" She was cut off by the sound of the front door closing. Her dad called out, "Heather, I'm home!"

"I can't talk about this anymore," Heather whispered. "Dad's home."

"Okay. We'll know if it's Brian tomorrow at school."

"How can you be so sure?"

Jamal giggled even louder. "If he was the guy who called he'll be extra-gross. He'll call you things like 'bat breath' and 'slug slime.' Otherwise he'll try to gross out Mark Matthew—just like always. Got it?"

"I think so," Heather said, hanging up. But she wasn't so sure.

Her dad bent down to kiss her cheek. "How was your day?"

"Oh, the usual." Heather decided not to tell him about the telephone calls.

If the *Guinness Book of World Records* had a category "World's Greatest Worrier," her father, Mike Reynolds, would be listed as the winner. Heather thought it was because her mom had died three years ago from cancer. So now he had to worry for two parents.

Heather popped the last meatball into her mouth. "These are the best meatballs you've ever made."

Her dad glanced at the plastic-coated calendar on the wall. CAHOOTS CATERING COMPANY was printed across the top. "Guess the secret ingredient was a success," he said. "We'll use it for the florists' luncheon on Tuesday."

Heather licked her fingers. "What secret ingredient?"

"I substituted ground pork for ground beef."

She stared at him for a moment. *"What?"*

When he said, "Oops, sorry. I forgot," she waved him quiet. She raced to the kitchen sink and spit. But nothing came out. Chopped pig was already in the pit of her stomach.

"How could you forget?" she repeated all the way down the hall to the bathroom, where she spent fifteen minutes flossing—just in case ground pig was stuck between her teeth.

After chewing two antacid tablets, Heather made her dad promise to tape the ingredients of his appetizers to the refrigerator door. She hadn't had a slice of ham or bacon for two years—since she'd found out they came from animals that rolled in mud and ate garbage. Gross!

Half an hour later, Heather huddled over a half-finished jigsaw puzzle. Puzzles were sort of a family tradition. A card table was always set up in the living room, topped with hundreds of colorful cardboard pieces.

Sometimes Heather put some of it together before school. Other times she and her dad worked on it after dinner while watching TV. Todd's only contribution was the puzzle's corners.

Mondays were the only quiet night in the Reynolds household. Her brother stayed at the library with Mr. Sánchez, his Spanish tutor, until ten o'clock. It was fun spending time alone with Dad. Too bad Todd couldn't be tutored in English, math and history the rest of the week.

"How many puzzles are left in the geography series?" Heather asked, fitting together several dark blue pieces. Oceans and lakes were the hardest because they all looked the same.

"We've finished five continents," her dad said. "So we still have two left. Plus the world globe."

Heather thought the easiest puzzle was the United States, since lots of the pieces had straight edges. She could put the whole thing together in less than an hour. And that was back in the fourth grade. It had helped her memorize all the state capitals. She'd gotten As in geography ever since.

Heather yawned and stretched. After fitting part of the Indian Ocean at the bottom tip of Australia, she said, "Good night, Daddy," and gave him a squeeze.

Her dad gathered her into a hug. "Sleep tight."

Heather trotted off to her room and changed into her flannel nightshirt. A few minutes later she was snuggling under her down comforter. Soon her thoughts drifted to the telephone call. Could Jamal be right? Could Brian Benson be the guy who'd called? She rolled over and punched the pillow. No way. Brian could get any girl in school—girls without birthmarks on their foreheads.

But a small voice inside her kept saying, "Maybe . . . just maybe . . ."

CHAPTER

2

Heather hammered on the bathroom door until her knuckles were purple. "Come on, Todd. It's eight-oh-seven. Seven whole minutes into *my* bathroom time."

The one day she needed extra time and Todd the Bathroom Hog attacked.

"Ple-e-e-ze!" she yelled.

Dad made two charts at the beginning of the school year. The chart for household chores was round like an extra-large pizza. Each wedge had a different chore: vacuuming, laundry, etc. The circle was rotated every month. That way no one got stuck mopping the kitchen two months in a row.

The bathroom chart worked the same way. One month Heather got the bathroom first thing in the morning. But at night she had to take her shower after Todd. Then it switched, and Todd got the bathroom first.

"Ple-e-e-ze!" she repeated. "I don't want to be late!"

Normally Heather spent only a few minutes in the morning hiding her birthmark. All she had to do was brush her bangs over her forehead. But on special occasions, like for school pictures, she patted it lightly with makeup.

She kept pounding on the door, thinking:

What if Brian was the guy who called?

What if he really does have a crush on me?

What if he wants to borrow something? I'd have to talk to him!

The blow-dryer finally stopped whirring. "What's the rush?" Todd said, opening the door. "School's not going anywhere."

Heather stared at him. "You're wearing a baseball cap! Why did you spend all that time on your hair if you were going to cover it up?"

"Not all my teachers let us wear caps in class, little sister." He punctuated his remark with a burp. It sounded like a sink draining.

Heather pushed into the bathroom and locked the door. She grabbed the jar of foundation from its secret hiding place: inside one of the rubber gloves under the sink. The other glove held mascara, eyeliner and shadow, plus a powdered blush —closeout items she'd picked up on sale. They were kept hidden because her dad wouldn't let her wear makeup, not even pale lipstick, until she was in junior high. Another whole year!

Heather poured a dot of Naked Beige into her palm and dabbed her forehead. Then she brushed it lightly with powder. At the last minute she decided to plaster her bangs in place with hairspray.

No way Brian Benson will see my artichoke today!

Just thinking about him made her stomach flutter. His eyes were as blue as peacock feathers. And he had a deep bronze suntan. Could he really be the guy who'd called? Part of her couldn't believe such a popular guy would like her. But part of her believed in the old saying "anything's possible."

She brushed her teeth, flossed *and* gargled—just in case she had a touch of pig breath.

On the way to school, Dad hummed along with the radio. He always listened to oldies stations. Both Heather and Todd could sing all the Beatles and Beach Boys songs in their sleep.

Dad started to slow down two blocks from the junior high school. Todd didn't like his friends to see him being dropped off. "So, Heather?" Dad asked. "Are you excited about the summer softball league?"

Heather smiled at the thought of softball season. She'd played shortstop on the Parks & Rec team for two years. Last year they had come in second. "Yeah," she said. "Practice starts in a few weeks."

"Would you like to go to a professional game this summer?" Dad asked.

"A major-league game?" Todd called from the backseat. "Can I ask a friend?"

Heather groaned at the sound of her brother's voice. Still, a major-league baseball game sounded like a blast. Especially if she could invite Jamal.

"You can both ask someone," Dad said.

Todd jumped out of the car as soon as it stopped. "Smell ya later!" he hollered over his shoulder.

A few minutes later, Dad was following a yellow bus into Heather's school parking lot. "Chelsey and I are thinking about expanding our business."

Chelsey Morris, her dad's business partner, lived across town in a two-story condominium. The entire downstairs had been converted into a commercial kitchen.

"Expanding it?" Heather asked. "How?"

"To include a bakery," Dad said. "We could make cakes for the parties we cater. Even cakes for parties we don't cater. What do you think?"

"That's a great idea," she said. "If it's a success, can we look for an apartment with an extra bathroom?"

Dad braked at the curb in front of the administration building. "Is it that bad?"

"You know how I feel about lima beans? Pickled beets? Ground pig? Imagine them all mixed up in the same casserole," Heather said with a shudder. "It's ten zillion times worse."

"Not a pretty picture," he said.

Heather slipped out of the front seat. "Thanks for the ride," she said, then headed up the sidewalk. Mr. Tsao's sixth-grade class was in the bungalow on the other side of the softball field. She broke into a trot when the five-minute bell rang.

Jamal was waiting for Heather in front of the door to the sixth-grade room. She dug her hand into her pocket and brought out a couple of mints without wrappers. "I thought you'd never get here. Everyone is already in class. At least the important kids." She giggled and the colorful beads on her black braids bounced. "If you know *who* I mean."

Heather picked the lint off the mint and

popped it in her mouth. "I'm so nervous," she said, thinking about the phone call. "This is worse than the first day of school."

"Are you girls coming inside?" Mr. Tsao smiled from the doorway. "It's almost time for class to start."

"Yes, sir," Heather said. But Jamal just giggled and followed her friend inside.

Heather shuffled down the aisle, past a pair of high-top sneakers with fluorescent laces. Brian Benson's shoes. All the little pigs in her stomach were doing cartwheels.

I hope it was Brian who called last night, she thought as she slid into her chair. *But what should I say to him? Should I let him know I know? Or should I act dumb?*

Her eyes locked on the back of his chair. She slowly raised her gaze to his baseball cap. He was wearing it backward. PARTY ANIMAL was stitched across the front.

When the cap turned she sucked in a bunch of air. It spouted into a hiccup. "Looks like you ironed your bangs instead of your clothes," he said, pointing to her stiffly sprayed bangs. "Or did you sleep on your face?"

"I—ummm," she stammered, and shot a glance at Jamal. Is this what Jamal had meant by "he'll be extra-gross"? Even though Jamal was two rows over, she must've heard every word. She gave Heather a double thumbs-up.

Big-Mouth Mark Matthews leaned across the aisle. He blew Cocoa Krispies breath in Heather's face. "It looks like you fell into a can of varnish," he said.

Heather glared at him. "Oh yeah?" She tapped her desk while thinking of a comeback. "And your head's as pointed as Spock's ears."

The bell rang and Mr. Tsao took the roll. Heather didn't hear her name at first. Mr. Tsao must've called it a bunch of times, because when she said "What?" all eyes were on her. She felt the heat creep up her neck as she slid down in her seat and mumbled "Here."

Each morning started off with a half hour in the vocabulary workbook. Blanks were filled in with answers about suffixes and prefixes. Lines were drawn connecting the week's spelling words to their definitions.

Heather scribbled on a scrap of notebook paper instead.

Dear Jamal:
I'm all mixed up! Brian was really gross. Just like you said. But so was Mark the Mouth. Help!

Confused in Class

Heather raised her hand. "Mr. Tsao? May I use the pencil sharpener?"

Mr. Tsao turned from the chalkboard, where he was setting up math problems. "Yes, Heather," he said, pushing his glasses back up his nose. "Go ahead."

When Heather walked around Brian's desk, he tried to trip her. On a normal day she would have stomped on his foot. Today she didn't know what to do. She hurried to the pencil sharpener and dropped the note on Jamal's desk.

Two minutes later a folded piece of paper landed in her lap.

Dear Confused:
Mark the Mouth doesn't count. He was just being a copycat. Brian's the one who insulted you first—so he's the one who likes you! Don't be surprised if you get another call after school today. This time don't hang up!

Love,
Your bestest friend

Heather felt all bubbly inside. She'd never had a real boyfriend before. Oh, sure, there had been dumb crushes in the fourth and fifth grades, but she'd been just a little kid so none of them counted.

A picture of her and Brian paired on school projects popped into her head. They stood together in the fire drill line and were partners in the science fair. She even saw him in the stands at one of her softball games, cheering her on with stomps and whistles.

Maybe someday Brian would give her a ring. Last year her brother had given Summer Thompson a ring. It didn't have diamonds or rubies. It was a plastic ring from a box of Cracker Jack. Still, Summer had worn it on her finger.

While the rest of the class matched vocabulary words, Heather drew a giant heart on the inside cover of her notebook. She formed Brian's initials with balloon letters. Then she added her initials.

Just as she started the arrow, Brian whispered over his shoulder, "I bet you sprayed your hair with deodorant. And shot your armpits with hairspray."

Heather smiled to herself. *He really does like me!*

After vocabulary and math, Mr. Tsao asked, "Does anyone have a current event to share?"

Mr. Tsao's current events weren't like those in other classes. No newspaper or magazine clippings. No reviews of TV news programs. Current events in Mr. Tsao's class were about the kids.

But he didn't allow negative stuff. No "I fell off my skateboard and sprained my ankle." No "Our guppies swam down the drain when Mom cleaned the fishbowl." Everything had to be positive.

Amy Crabtree had spent half an hour picking up trash in front of the dance studio. Jay Arnold had collected aluminum cans from his neighbors and donated the money to the Red Cross. Brandon Kamp had signed up to plant seedling trees at the city park.

"Those are all terrific current events," Mr. Tsao said. "Anyone else?"

Brian Benson raised his hand. "I went to my grandparents' house after school yesterday," he said. "We spent all afternoon replacing old boards in their barn. It took four hours, but we finished the job."

Heather and Jamal exchanged glances. *Then it wasn't Brian Benson!*

Heather tried not to show her disappointment. She had started to believe Brian had made the calls, that the most popular guy in the sixth grade liked her.

She closed her eyes and dropped her head in her hands. This was quickly becoming one of the worst days in her life.

CHAPTER

3

When school was over, the sun was as hot as a curling iron. Heather tied the sleeves of her sweatshirt around her waist. She pushed her bangs off her sweaty forehead, and makeup rubbed off on her hand. Who cared? There wasn't any reason to hide her artichoke now.

"I'm so stupid," Heather said to Jamal. She kicked at a rock on the sidewalk. "For five minutes I thought Brian Benson liked me. Why would he like me? He can have any girl in class. Besides, I have a vegetable on my face."

Jamal snapped a Frisbee-size peanut-butter cookie in two. "Most kids don't notice your birthmark," she said, handing Heather the bigger piece of cookie. "Or they just don't pay any attention to it."

Heather chewed with her mouth open. "What if it starts to grow? In junior high it'll be the size of a softball . . . in high school it'll be the size of a basketball. By college I'll be one big pink artichoke."

Jamal laughed. "Come on, Heather. Stop exaggerating. We've been best friends since the first grade. It's the same size it's always been."

Heather smiled at her. "Thanks."

They stopped on the corner and waited for the traffic sign to flash WALK. Jamal followed Heather along the crosswalk line. "Look on the bright side," she said. "You *still* have a secret admirer."

"Huh-uh. No way. It was a crank call. That's all," Heather said. "The guy probably found our number in the phone book. So it wasn't even anyone I know. I want to forget the whole thing."

Jamal jumped in front of her. "How can you forget about a secret admirer? It's the most romantic—"

Heather drowned her out by reciting the preamble to the Constitution, which they had recently had to memorize.

Jamal threw up her hands. "Okay. We'll forget it."

A few minutes later they reached the corner where they split off to go their separate ways. "Later," they both said.

Heather's apartment building was in the center of the block. She skipped every other step going up the two flights of stairs and pulled a key from her backpack. The stereo in the living room blasted Watermelon Seed's new song, "Together We Jam."

She found her brother in the kitchen in a steamy mess. Two pots bubbled on the stove. Graters, strainers and knives littered the counters.

Todd was slumped over the sink, wiping tears from his eyes. "Can you help me?" he cried.

Heather rushed over. "What's wrong? Did you cut yourself?"

He blotted his eyes and pointed to the cutting board. Half a chopped onion topped it. "Can you give me a hand?" he repeated. "I know it's my night to cook, but I have soccer practice."

"Onions," she said, and gave him a playful punch. "Is that all?"

Todd scraped the onions into some bubbling orange stuff—melted cheddar cheese. "I wish Dad would let us make macaroni and cheese from a package," he said, stirring the orange mess. "It's a lot easier than making it from scratch. And faster too."

"I'll help wash some of this stuff," Heather said, "while the macaroni boils."

Heather scrubbed the utensils and handed them to Todd to be dried. After he shoved the last measuring spoon into a drawer, he dumped the strained noodles into a casserole dish and stirred in the melted cheese.

"Can you bake it for me?" Todd asked, reaching for his soccer ball. "Three-fifty for thirty minutes."

"If I can have the bathroom first in the morning," she called after him.

"It's a deal," he said, slamming the front door.

Heather gathered the wet dishtowels, including one tossed over the answering machine. That's when she noticed the blinking amber light. She hit the Play button and listened to the messages.

"Heather? This is Amy. Did we have homework in geography? I forget. Give me a call, okay? I'll be home from rehearsal after eight."

Heather smiled. Kids always called about geography homework. They knew she got As in geography.

Beep.

"Hello, Michael." It was Chelsey, Dad's business partner. "I thought of another name for the bakery. How do you like 'Bake Somebody Happy'? Oh, shoot. This is the apartment phone, right? I'll call back and leave a message on the business phone."

This time Heather laughed. Chelsey still mixed up the business number with the apartment number. The whole reason Dad had had a second phone installed in his bedroom was so that he wouldn't miss his business calls. Todd was lousy at taking messages. And sometimes Heather forgot to write them down.

Beep.

Heather leaned closer to listen to the next message.

"Ummm, hi. It's me again."

"You?" Even though there wasn't any static on the line, she knew it was the crank caller.

"Okay, I'll admit it. I was bored—with a capital *B*. That's the only reason I called," he rambled on. "Otherwise I would've had to tackle my homework. Besides, I didn't expect a kid to answer." Heather listened with her mouth hanging open. "See, the phone book was open to *Food Service.* Mom had circled a bunch of caterers, so I thought of the pigs' feet riddle. Why did you answer, anyway? Isn't this a business number?"

Heather couldn't believe he'd called back—and put such a long message on the answering machine. Especially since she hadn't been friendly before.

There was a short pause. "If you ever get

bored doing homework, it's okay to call me. You can even tell me dumb jokes. My number is 555-2458. Ummm, if anyone else gets this message, just ignore it. Okay?"

Beep.

Heather rewound the tape and played it again. The voice belonged to a kid, but it wasn't anyone from class. Or the apartment building. In fact, she was 150 percent sure she didn't know him. So why should he care whether she'd hung up on him?

Heather listened to the tape another six times. "It's okay to call me . . . My number is . . ." She grabbed the phone and poked in seven numbers. "Hello, Mrs. Jacobson. Is Jamal there?"

"She'll be back in an hour or so," Jamal's mother answered. "She went to the grocery store with her dad."

"Ple-e-e-ze tell her to call as soon as she comes in. It's a *humongous* emergency."

Heather hung up. *Maybe I will call him. To tell him how much trouble he caused me. First I had to go into Todd's room to answer the phone. Then I acted like an idiot at school . . . plus the notes traded with Jamal. What if Mr. Tsao had seen us? We'd both be in detention. And my bangs must've looked like a Brillo pad!*

A picture of Brian Benson flashed in her head. She saw the whopping balloon letters scratched inside her notebook—in purple ink. "I was such a dope!" she shouted at the phone. "All because of a crank call!"

Heather punched in the first numbers as if she were squashing bugs, then froze. *What will I say if someone else answers? "Is the crank caller home?" "Can I talk to Mr. Boredom?"*

She sucked in a deep breath and finished dialing the numbers. The phone rang one, two, three times. Finally someone picked up. "Hello?" It was the voice.

Her mouth was as dry as a plain peanut-butter sandwich.

"Who's there?"

Finally she blurted, "I don't care if you were

bored stiffer than a surfboard. If you call again I'm turning you in to the FBI. The CIA. And the . . . the . . . IRS!"

"Yeah, it was dumb," he said. "Riddles are for little kids."

"Huh?" she said, thrown off guard. When she had an argument with her brother, he always fought back. "What did you say?"

"I didn't think a kid would answer the phone," he said. "Isn't this a business number? Cahoots Catering. That's what it said in the phone book—"

"Do you know how much trouble you caused me?" Heather cut in. "First I had to go into my brother's room to get the phone. That alone is worse than a living nightmare." She shuddered. "Then I thought . . . I mean, Jamal thought . . . We both thought you were someone in my class."

"Really? Where do you go to school?"

"Why should I tell you anything?"

"I'm in the seventh grade," he went on. "I go

33

to M. L. King Junior High. As in Martin Luther."

"One of my brother's friends goes to M. L. King." Heather wondered if he was still jabbering so he wouldn't have to do homework. Then she caught herself and said, "Hey, wait a minute. Don't try to change the subject."

"You sound like you're in the seventh grade too. Or maybe the eighth. Am I right?"

Heather liked the idea of being in junior high. But she said, "You can't trick me like that."

"I'm not trying to trick you. I was just wondering, that's all. What's the big deal?"

Heather sucked in a deep breath.

"What's your name, anyway?"

"Ms. None of Your Business!"

"I'll tell you mine. It's Justin." When she didn't answer, he went on, "What do you do when you're bored?"

"Sometimes I talk on the phone," she admitted. "But I don't call strangers. I call my best friend."

"Me too. But one of my friends just moved.

And my other friend has strep throat. He might have to have his tonsils out."

Heather felt herself start to weaken. Maybe she had overreacted—just a little. "An operation? That's too bad."

Their conversation bounced back and forth like a tennis ball. Justin whacked out a bunch of questions. Heather chased them and whacked them back.

Heather explained about the phone number. "Dad used to have this phone for business," she said. "But he decided he needed a separate number. He changed it on his business cards and in newspaper ads. But the home number is still in the business section of the phone book."

"That's cuz the phone book only comes out once a year," Justin said.

"Yeah, right."

They talked and talked about all sorts of things. Their favorite foods, TV shows, rock stars. Schools and teachers. Parents and friends. Sports and hobbies. Even their best subjects in school.

"What's your favorite sport?" Justin asked.

"I'm on the school softball team," she told him. "Last year I played shortstop."

"Really? I'm on the baseball team," he said. "I'm the catcher."

Before long the pigs' feet riddle had faded from Heather's mind. She even forgot about Brian Benson.

"My stepbrother is an alien from outer space," Justin said. "He makes triple-decker sandwiches out of refried beans."

Heather shuddered. "That's as sick as Todd's peanut-butter-and-cucumber sandwiches. With ketchup."

"Gross!"

When the front door slammed, Heather glanced at the kitchen clock. "We've been on the phone for almost an hour," she said, then laughed. "That's one of the reasons Dad got a different number for his business. Well . . . guess I'd better get going."

"Is it okay if I call again sometime?" Justin asked.

"If you promise not to ask any riddles," Heather said. Then she added, "I just broke Dad's number-one rule."

"What's that?" Justin asked.

"Never talk to strangers."

This time they both laughed. Even though she'd never met Justin, she was starting to think of him as a friend. A telephone friend. *What's wrong with that?* she asked herself. *Not a thing.*

Heather couldn't wait to tell Jamal.

CHAPTER
4

The week after the crank call zipped by faster than any one of Heather's favorite TV shows. At first Justin only called her when none of his other friends was home. And Heather only called him when Jamal had gone somewhere. But after several days they were calling for no particular reason—just to talk.

Jamal kept saying, "Gosh, Heather. We never talk on the phone anymore. Your line's always busy." Then she'd giggle. "This is more romantic than a soap opera."

"It is *not* romantic," Heather would repeat. "We're friends. We talk about normal stuff. What we're doing in school. What we did over summer vacation. Did I tell you he went to Alaska? And took a boat ride to a glacier?"

"About a hundred times."

"There's nothing romantic about frozen water."

A few days later, Heather was slumped over the card table putting together pieces of the Great Barrier Reef. Her dad strolled into the living room and pulled up a chair. "Looks like we might finish the puzzle this week," he said.

Heather pointed to the long, skinny piece she'd been working on. "Is the Barrier Reef on the East Coast?"

Dad nodded. "Sure is."

They worked on the puzzle together without saying anything for several minutes. Soon her dad started to fidget in his chair. "So . . . tell me about your new friend," he said slowly. "His name is Justin. Right?"

Heather snapped the last section of the reef into place. "He's just a guy, Dad. That's all."

"I figured that," he said. "How old is he?"

"Just a year older than I am," she said.

"Where does he go to school?" Dad asked next. "Does he live around here?"

Heather repeated some of the stuff she'd been telling Jamal. "Don't be such a worrywart," she added. "Next year we'll be at the same school. Todd would go to M. L. King if they had a soccer team. Besides, he's just a friend." She paused, thinking about it. "A telephone friend."

Dad's sigh sounded like air escaping from a balloon. "Okay," he finally gave in. "Just don't spend *all* your time on the phone."

Heather draped her arm over his shoulder. "I won't."

The following week Jamal was in Heather's kitchen doing homework. The small television set on the counter was tuned to an afternoon talk show about married couples who had met on blind dates.

The clock built into the double oven said fifteen minutes before four. Justin usually made the afternoon call, since he came home from school later than she did—any minute now.

Heather answered the phone on the first ring. "Hi, Justin. What's happening?"

Jamal turned up the TV just as the host was saying, "Then it was love at first sight?"

Heather's look was hot enough to melt butter. Jamal adjusted the volume and went back to her math homework. Every few minutes she made kissy noises. Heather just glared at her.

Jamal scribbled a note and slid it across the counter. "Ask him what he looks like." Heather read it and shoved it back. "Just ask him how tall he is." Heather shook her head. But the notes kept coming. "What color are his eyes?" "What color is his hair?" "What kind of car do his parents drive?"

Heather finally wrote back, "Just one question. Then stop bugging me!"

Jamal's eyes widened as she scooted closer.

"Ummm, Justin . . ." Heather stopped, embarrassed. "Well, we've been friends for almost two weeks. I know it's silly . . . but I don't know what you look like."

"I was sort of wondering the same thing." There was an awkward silence before he said, "I bet your hair's light. Maybe even blond. And probably straight. Am I right?"

Heather squinted at her bangs. They were the same color as burned toast. Dark brown. Most of the time her hair was straight—except when it rained. Then it curled into frizzy balls. "That's a good guess." She hadn't lied exactly—she just hadn't told the truth.

"And your eyes. Let's see. Are they green?"

Her eyes matched her dull brown hair. "How did you know?"

In another two minutes she'd painted herself as a tall blonde with green eyes and straight teeth. Even the last part was untrue. In six months she'd be wearing braces, but only on top. She squirmed on the stool. *Why didn't I tell him the truth?*

"Do you want to guess about me?" Justin asked.

Heather covered the mouthpiece and whispered, "He wants me to guess."

Jamal scribbled, "Tall. Dark. Hunk."

Heather rolled her eyes. Jamal watched too many soap operas. And too many talk shows. This entire conversation was her fault!

"Is your hair dark? I don't mean black. Kind of like hot chocolate before the marshmallows have melted."

"You got it."

"Really?" Heather was surprised. She was usually rotten at guessing games. "Are you tall? Not flagpole tall," she added quickly. She didn't want him to feel bad if his height was average. "Sort of medium tall."

"Right again. Er, hold on a minute." Heather listened while he told his mother he'd help her with a few chores. "I gotta go. I'll talk to you later."

"Later," Heather said before hanging up. "He

is a tall, dark hunk," she said to Jamal. "And he thinks I'm blond with green eyes. I don't know why I lied." She looked as if she might throw up. "It's a good thing he'll never see me."

"Come on," Jamal said. "He wasn't telling you the truth. He was making it up, just like you were."

Heather chewed on a strand of hair. "No way. Believe me. Justin wouldn't lie."

"Everyone tells white lies," Jamal insisted. "Especially adolescents. It was on last week's episode of *The Young and the Dissatisfied*. Remember?"

"No, not Justin Steamer."

"Wanna bet?"

Heather smoothed her bangs over her birthmark. It would be a relief if Justin was a normal kid. Maybe he wore glasses or braces—or walked with a limp. "How can we find out?"

Jamal was already flipping through the phone book. "Didn't you say his last name is Steamer? Or is that his stepfather's name?"

"It's his name, too."

"S-T-E-A . . . Here it is. One-twenty-five Foothill Lane. That's only a couple of miles from here," Jamal said. "What are we waiting for?" They carried their in-line skates and helmets to the ground floor, put them on and skated off.

It should have taken only half an hour to skate to Foothill Lane, but Heather kept stopping to practice crossovers. One time she jumped the same curb six times. She suddenly wished she was home in bed. With a pillow over her head.

Two blocks later she stood across the street from 125. "That's it." She stared at the two-story condominium. "Now what?"

"We wait."

Jamal ducked behind a thick hedge on their side of the street. Heather joined her. They used their helmets to prop several branches apart. Except for a few large leaves, they had a clear view of Justin's home.

Heather had just made her fists into binoculars when something poked her from behind. "What the—?" She spun around to find a large dog with a Frisbee in his mouth. He dropped it and barked.

Jamal giggled. "He wants to play."

The dog acted as if he understood. He barked even more loudly.

"Shhh!" Heather shushed him. She tossed the Frisbee down the street, and the dog scampered off.

"Don't look now," Jamal said, "but someone's coming out of the house."

Heather looked as if she might faint. "Is it Justin?"

His hair was almost black and buzzed short on top. The sides were long enough to be slicked back over his ears. Even though they weren't that close, Jamal thought he wore a gold stud in one ear. Heather thought it was a mole.

Jamal lowered her voice. "I hope I'm right."

Heather nodded. "Me too."

Justin carried a grease-stained sack to the barrels at the curb. He was dropping the sack into a barrel when something drew his attention across the street. He stared straight at the hedge. "What's going on?"

Heather and Jamal exchanged glances. *Can he see us?*

Justin bounced off the curb. "What do you think you're doing?"

Jamal whispered, "What are we going to do?"

Heather shot a quick glance in her direction, but she couldn't answer. Her throat was too dry.

Justin continued to stroll across the street. "How'd you get out, anyway?"

The dog barked.

"Come on, E.T. Let's go home."

Heather didn't recover until Justin disappeared into his house. "Whew! Talk about a close one!"

Jamal grinned. "You were right. Justin doesn't tell white lies. He is a hunk."

Heather looked at her, horrified. "How can we be friends?" she said as soon as she recovered her voice. "Now that I know Justin's a ten and I'm barely a five? Less if you deduct points for artichokes."

CHAPTER
5

Todd stumbled past the kitchen carrying a basket of dirty clothes. It was his turn to do the laundry. "Think I'll put a load in before soccer practice," he said.

Heather almost fainted—her training bra was swinging over the edge of the basket. She must have accidentally left it in the bathroom after her shower the night before. "I've told you a zillion times!" she shouted. "I don't want you washing my clothes!"

Todd waved the bra. "Is this yours? I thought it was a slingshot." He steadied the basket against the couch and used the bra to shoot a balled-up sock at the TV set.

"Daddy! Make him stop!"

Dad was bent over the kitchen counter, deep in a cookbook called *California Cuisine*.

Todd hooked the bra over the doorknob before heading to the laundry room. "Bra-bra-bo-bra . . . ," he sang down the hall.

"Dad!"

Dad mumbled something about marinated bean curd.

Heather stuffed her bra into the pocket of her pj's and returned to the kitchen. She slumped over a bowl of cornflakes, staring at the phone. How could she talk to Justin now? Knowing he was a ten? And she was just an average kid? If she stared at the phone long enough, maybe it would disappear.

Instead of disappearing, it rang. She sucked in enough air to choke a dinosaur. It had to be Justin. No one else called this early on Saturday morning.

Ring.

She slumped even lower on the stool. *What will I say to him?* she wondered as the phone continued to ring. *By the way, Justin. There's something I have to tell you. I really have grocery-bag-brown hair. It's past my shoulders, only because I pull on it a hundred times every night. My eyes are the color of dirt clods. And I have an artichoke on my forehead.*

Ring.

Dad glanced up from the cookbook. "Aren't you going to get that?"

Just as she exaggerated a yawn and said, "I'm not awake yet," the machine clicked on.

A few seconds later, Justin's voice spilled into the kitchen. "Heather? Are you still asleep? Bummer. Call me as soon as you get up. I have something to tell you. It's superimportant!"

Beep.

Dad poured himself a cup of coffee. "You and Justin have been on the phone constantly for the last two weeks." He cleared his throat with an *uh-humm*. "And I emphasize the word *constantly*. Suddenly you're too tired to talk to him? What gives?"

Heather looked away from the phone. "It's sort of personal."

Her father rested on the stool next to her. "Maybe I can help."

"Not this time," she said.

"Come on, Heather. Haven't I helped you with problems before?" he asked. "Remember when you left your mitt in the locker room at Hanford? Didn't I drive two hours the next day to pick it up?"

Heather nodded.

"What about the time your volcano collapsed?" he went on. "We ended up molding the papier-mâché around a fondue pot. And your teacher lit the candle just before the judges came in."

Heather cracked a smile, recalling her science fair project of two years before. "The volcano looked like it was about to erupt," she said. "I got an A-plus."

"See? Maybe I can help this time too."

Heather slurped a bite of soggy cornflakes,

thinking. "You and Mom were friends before you started dating, weren't you?" she asked.

Dad nodded over his coffee. "Good friends."

Thinking about her mother still made Heather sad. Mostly because she missed her so much. At least now it wasn't the kind of sadness that made her cry. "What if Mom hadn't been pretty?" she said slowly. "Would you have been such good friends? I mean, what if she had a flaw? Would you have started talking to her in the first place?"

"A flaw? Like a birthmark?" Dad smiled. "Is that what's bothering you?"

"It's not funny!"

"I'm not laughing *at* you," he said gently. "But no one notices your birthmark."

Heather shoved her half-eaten bowl of cereal across the table. Milk slopped over the side. She drew an upside-down smile in the puddle.

"You're just saying that because you don't want me to feel bad."

"I *don't* want you to feel bad. That's true," he said. "But I'm also saying it because I mean it."

"Really?"

"Swear on a stack of cookbooks," he said, and gave her a warm squeeze. "Now, finish your breakfast. And stop being such a worrywart."

She squeezed him back. Wasn't it just last week that she'd called him a worrywart? "Thanks, Dad," she said, and he returned to *California Cuisine*.

Heather slurped the rest of her cereal and rinsed her bowl before putting it in the dishwasher. *Thank goodness Dad didn't spout the Don't Judge a Book by Its Cover speech*. She'd heard it so many times she had it memorized: "Anyone who doesn't want to be your friend because of the way you look doesn't deserve to be your friend."

She wanted to believe it. She *did* believe it. At least most of the time. But did everyone else believe it? More important: Did Justin S. Steamer believe it?

If only Justin didn't look like a rock star, she thought. *If he was just a regular kid, then I wouldn't be so self-conscious.*

These thoughts bounced around in her head as

she went to her room. She plopped on her unmade bed and ripped a piece of paper from her
notebook. It was time to compose a new message
for the answering machine.

The words tumbled out on the paper. "Hi.
This is the Reynolds residence. Michael and
Todd are out at the moment. Heather has lar-
yngitis. Please leave your message at . . ."
She scratched that out and started over.
"Heather joined a foreign-exchange program.
Please leave a message at the sound of the
beep. She'll call you when she returns from
Tasmania."

Heather rolled over and remembered all the
things she and Justin had talked about in the past
two weeks. It was amazing how much they had in
common. Justin hated sharing a bedroom with
his stepbrother, whom he described as a three-
toed sloth. She hated sharing a bathroom with
her brother, Todd the Hog. That's when their
first secret had been shared: Each wanted to be
an only child.

They even talked about serious stuff. How he

had felt when his parents were divorced. How she had felt when her mother had died. They'd both cried every night for months.

Heather realized she knew more about Justin than she did about some of her relatives. She didn't know Aunt Shannon's favorite TV show. She didn't know Grandma Stovall's favorite book. She didn't even know who her cousins cheered for in the Super Bowl.

But she knew all these things—and lots more —about Justin S. Steamer.

"Heather?" Her dad knocked on the door. "Justin's on the phone."

"Justin who?"

"Heather!"

"Okay," she moaned. "I'm coming."

She grabbed a baseball cap, yanked the bill over her forehead and plodded down the hall. "Yo, Justin," she muttered. "What's happening?"

"Ummm . . . er . . . not much. How 'bout you?"

His voice sounded weird. Something was

wrong. Maybe he *had* seen them hiding behind the hedge.

"Has your mail come yet?" he asked.

"Not yet. Why?"

"The three-toed sloth has struck again." His voice cracked. "He got your address from the phone book. And sent you an invitation to my birthday party. Without even asking me."

"That was stupid," Heather said. But she was thinking, *Why wouldn't you want me to come to your party?*

"Not that I didn't want to invite you," he added quickly. "Because I did. I mean, I do. But I should've been the one to send it. Not Sloth-Foot. Anyway, the party's this Sunday at noon."

The day after tomorrow? Heather thought in a panic. More than her hands were sweaty.

"I just didn't want you to think you *had* to come. Especially since it'll be all relatives. Sort of a family gathering. You know how boring they are," he rattled on. "Besides, I didn't want you to think you *had* to buy me a present."

"But I *want* to get you something for your birthday," she blurted.

"You mean you want to come? Even with all my boring relatives?"

"Won't your best friend be there?" she asked. "The one who had strep?"

"He's having his tonsils out," Justin said.

"Oh."

Suddenly a picture of Justin popped into Heather's head. He was so handsome he belonged on the cover of a romance novel. She imagined them seated together at his birthday party.

What would he say when he found out she'd lied about her appearance? About the color of her eyes? Her hair? What would he say about her artichoke? Just thinking about these things gave her goose bumps.

"Heather? Are you there?"

Suddenly her brain went *Tilt*. She couldn't think of an excuse for not going to the party. At least one that didn't sound totally stupid.

"Heather?" he repeated.

Heather's sigh was long enough to blow out a hundred candles. "Yes," she said. "I'm here." How could she say no to his invitation without hurting his feelings?

CHAPTER

6

The next day Heather and Jamal were sprawled on Heather's living room floor in front of the TV. Jamal had just pushed a tape of *The Young and the Dissatisfied* into the VCR. During the week Jamal would tape all five episodes; then she and Heather would watch them together on the weekends. Heather was in charge of hot buttered popcorn, which she sprinkled with chocolate chips.

Heather fast-forwarded through a commercial. "I didn't mean to accept the invitation. It just sort of happened. I have to be at Rusty's Pizza Parlor tomorrow at noon—unless I come down with an infectious disease."

Jamal grabbed a handful of popcorn. She picked out the chocolate chips and ate them separately. "You didn't tell me it was tomorrow!"

"I'm still in shock."

"What're you going to wear?"

"Nothing—"

Jamal burst out laughing.

"I'm not going naked." Heather shot her a look. "I'm not going at all. You're going in my place. It'll be your first role as an actress."

"There's only one problem," Jamal said.

"What?"

"I'm black."

"Soooooo?"

"He thinks you have blond hair and green eyes," Jamal said with a silly grin.

Heather chewed a strand of hair. "Then I'll have to find a blond wig. And order colored contacts."

"You don't have time for any of that," Jamal said. "What you really need is a new outfit. Something that will knock his socks off."

"Yeah. So he won't notice any of the other stuff." She pushed Pause on the remote control. A young couple was frozen in a steamy embrace.

"Da-ad!" Heather stretched the word into two syllables. "May I borrow your credit card?"

A few moments later her dad strolled in from the kitchen. He wore his CHOP TILL YOU DROP apron. The smell of garlic covered him like an invisible cloud. "What's up?"

"Can I buy something for Justin's birthday party?" she asked.

Earlier in the morning she'd told him about Justin's party. After answering all the usual questions, he'd said she could go. Probably because she'd told him Justin's mom was a substitute teacher. For some reason he thought teachers were responsible.

"What did you want to get him?" Dad asked.

Heather and Jamal exchanged glances. *We forgot about a present!*

"Uh, I want to get him something," Heather

said. "I'm not sure what. But I want to wear something special. Is it okay? I haven't bought anything new since school started."

"How much do you need?" Dad asked.

"I don't know exactly what I want," Heather said.

Heather's father paused for a moment, then removed his wallet and unfolded a pink slip. "I have credit left from a sweater I returned. Would Dillon's Department Store have something?"

Heather stared at the slip. "Forty-five dollars?"

"You can bring me the change." Dad raised his eyebrows at the TV. "What are you kids watching?"

Heather pushed through the double doors of Dillon's Department Store. Jamal followed her down an aisle lined with mannequins in see-through lingerie, lace teddies and silk camisoles.

Formal Wear was squeezed between Lingerie and Cosmetics. Jamal stopped in front of a rack marked HALF PRICE. Heather picked out a dress solid with little silver mirrors. She squinted at her reflections. There were zillions of them. "If the power went out I'd glow in the dark."

Jamal checked a couple of price tags. "Do you know how much these cost? One hundred and fifty dollars!"

Heather exhaled loudly through her nose. It came out as a snort. When she looked across the store she saw a banner hanging in Cosmetics: SPECIAL $9.99 MAKEOVER WITH PURCHASE OF LIPSTICK.

Jamal followed her gaze. "What are we waiting for?"

The woman behind the counter could have won a Madonna look-alike contest. Her hair was bleached the color of French vanilla ice cream. Her name tag read ASHLEY. "Can I help you girls?" she asked.

Heather and Jamal traded looks, but neither one answered.

"Are you part of the fashion show?" Ashley asked. "The fund-raiser for the PTA?"

"Er, yeah," they both answered. "The fashion show."

Ashley smiled. "I've already done a couple of girls."

A moment later Heather was seated on a brass stool, her hair smoothed off her face with a headband. Ashley patted her face with a cotton ball saturated with something called a toner. Next she used little rubber things to blend the foundation.

"You're going to look super tomorrow," Jamal said.

"Isn't the fashion show tonight?" Ashley asked, without looking up.

"Um, well . . ." Jamal twirled a braid around her finger. "The dress rehearsal is tonight. But the official show isn't until tomorrow."

"Then you'd better sleep on your back," Ashley said, "so you won't smear your makeup."

"Good thinking," said Jamal.

A stroke of midnight-blue mascara followed sky-blue eye shadow. The final touch was blush streaked across Heather's cheeks. Ashley handed her a mirror. "What do you think?"

Heather stared wide-eyed at her reflection. "Is this really me?"

"Oh, Heather," Jamal said. "You look like a model!"

Heather couldn't believe it. Now *she* looked like she belonged on the cover of a romance novel. The best part was her birthmark. It had totally disappeared.

Ashley smiled. "Good luck with the show."

Heather paid for the makeover, plus a tube of Purple Passion lipstick. She shoved a revised credit slip into her pocket. There was more than enough left to buy a birthday present.

"Let's hit the CD department," she said to Jamal.

CHAPTER

7

Heather and Jamal rounded the corner to the garage under the apartment building. The CAHOOTS CATERING COMPANY van was backed up to the bottom of the stairwell. Both rear doors were open.

When Heather heard her dad humming she pulled Jamal behind a sports car. "We can't let him see me with all this makeup on," she whispered.

Heather watched while her dad slid a tray of appetizers onto a rack. She poked Jamal and pointed to the back stairs. Jamal nodded. They crept between two cars with their shopping bags held tightly against their chests.

"That was a close one," Heather said.

They ran into Todd in the next corridor. A pair of in-line skates bobbled over his shoulder, the laces tied in a knot. He was on his way to Cheap Thrills, a video-game arcade. "Hey, little sister. Looks like you're having a bad hair day. What happened to your face?"

"Ple-e-e-ze," she begged. "Don't tell Dad."

Todd cracked his gum. "What'll you give me?"

"Why should I *give* you anything?" she asked. "I helped you with dinner. Remember? It wasn't even my turn to cook."

"That was two weeks ago," Todd said, continuing down the hall. "Besides, I let you have the bathroom first. My room could use a good scrubdown."

Heather grunted. "I'd rather eat sausage casing."

Heather and Jamal disappeared up the back stairs. A few minutes later they were inside the apartment—in the bathroom with the door locked. Thank goodness Jamal's mother had said she could spend the night. Heather needed her moral support more than ever!

"Do you think it'll stay like this?" Heather studied herself in the mirror. "Until tomorrow?"

Jamal nodded. "If you sleep on your back."

A knock on the door made them both jump. "Todd told me you were home." It was Heather's dad. "How was shopping? Did you find something? When can I have a fashion show?"

Heather shot Jamal a look. "Ummm, can I show you later?"

"I'm leaving in a few minutes. It's the Shaymans' anniversary party. I should be home by nine-thirty. Open the door so I can say good-bye."

His words stretched out and slapped her in the face. "We're sort of busy," she said in a shaky voice.

"Then how about a quick hug?" he asked.

"But Dad"—she paused to think of another tactic—"Jamal's just getting into the shower."

There was a long pause before he said, "Then I'll see you after the party. Call Mrs. Jensen if you need anything."

Heather leaned against the hamper, relieved. "Don't worry about us, Dad. We're just going to watch a movie."

Heather waited for the sound of the front door closing before she unlocked the bathroom door. She counted to ten before cracking it open. "Dad?" No answer. "Dad?" Still no answer.

Jamal peeked out. "The coast is clear."

There were four and a half episodes of *The Young and the Dissatisfied* left to watch. Jamal opened a package of New Nails, her contribution to the makeover effort. She spread ten tips on the carpet in front of the TV. Heather brought in the glue.

Heather's nails had to be filed first. Jamal then dabbed the ends with glue and set each plastic tip in place. "These are awesome," Heather said when her right hand was finished.

That was when the inside of her nose started to itch. Without thinking, she scratched it.

The scream that followed was sharp enough to pop balloons.

"What am I going to do?"

"Take your finger out of your nose."

Heather glared at her. "It's stuck. It's *glued.* Quick. Look on the label. Maybe it tells how to get it off skin."

Jamal was studying the fine print when the phone rang.

"D-D-Don't answer it," Heather stammered. "No. Wait a minute. It might be Dad calling to check on us."

Ring.

"You answer it. Tell him I'm . . . I'm indisposed." As in "rendered unfit." They'd had that word in spelling. It could also mean to be ill, like she felt now.

"He'll still want to talk to you," Jamal said.

Heather skidded across the kitchen floor and grabbed the phone before the machine clicked on. "Hello?" she said, holding the phone with her left hand. "Er, hi, Justin."

Jamal bounced from one foot to the other, as if

she might wet her pants. "It's *Justin*?" She slapped both hands over her mouth. Giggles seeped between her fingers.

"I wanted to warn you about some of my relatives," Justin said. "Since you'll be stuck with them tomorrow at the party."

Heather shuddered at the word *stuck*.

Justin jabbered on, "Do you have paper and a pencil?"

"Ummm, sure." Paper and pencil! How was she supposed to write with her finger up her nose?

"Don't even talk to the three-toed sloth," Justin said. "He spends his allowance on Magic By Mail. His favorite trick used to be rubber barf. But our dog chewed it up."

"Okay." Heather hardly heard him. She was trying to wiggle her finger, but it wouldn't budge.

"He got a package a couple of days ago," Justin went on. "I don't know what it is. Probably something for the party. Something gross."

What would Justin think if he knew her finger was in her nose? Talk about gross!

Justin spent the next ten minutes warning her about aunts, uncles and cousins. "My aunt has a voice that sounds like screeching tires," he said, "so you might want to wear earplugs."

Heather wiggled her finger again. Nothing.

"One of my uncles tells the dumbest jokes. Worse than riddles." Then he said, "Mom isn't too bad. I hope she wears normal clothes, not oversized sweats. Otherwise she looks like a deflated beach ball." He ended by saying, "Just ignore everyone."

Heather mumbled, "Okay."

"Huh?" he asked. "Your voice sounds kind of funny. You're not catching a cold, are you?"

Justin's words crackled over the phone. Heather felt a sneeze coming on. Her eyes fluttered and she took short, shallow breaths. "Ah, ah, ah . . ."

Jamal shoved her finger under Heather's nose. "Ahhhh, sh-o-o-o-o!" Heather sneezed into the receiver. Her finger stayed stuck in her nose.

"Sounds like a cold to me," Justin said. "You'd better make a cup of herbal tea with lemon and honey."

Heather's eyes watered. Her nose tickled. And she felt like a total idiot. "Okay," she muttered.

"I'll call later to see how you're feeling," he said.

Heather nodded and said, "Uh-huh," then wiped her nose on a napkin.

After they said "See you," Heather turned back to Jamal. "What am I going to do?"

Jamal giggled. "The label says to use nail polish remover."

As soon as she daubed Heather's nose with a saturated cotton swab, the glue loosened up. Heather removed the rest of the fake fingernails. She wasn't taking any chances on another freak accident.

Jamal still insisted on applying two coats of polish to Heather's stubby nails. Candy Apple Red. Then she fanned Heather's nails with the hair dryer.

It was getting late. Jamal whirled through the

apartment gathering up all the evidence, while Heather wrote her dad a note. It said, "We went to bed early. Hope your party was a success. See you in the morning." A string of *X*s and *O*s underlined her signature.

"Don't roll over," Jamal warned before they climbed into bed, "or you'll mess up your face."

Heather settled into her pillow and listened while Jamal oozed about Mark the Mouth. Heather didn't understand it. Just last week he'd raised his hand to ask if *gross-out* was one word or two. A total airhead.

Then her thoughts drifted to the next day. The party started at noon. How could she avoid Dad all morning? He'd never let her out of the apartment if he saw her wearing eye makeup and lipstick. She suddenly felt like the center of one of his soufflés—ready to collapse if someone made a loud noise.

She nudged Jamal and whispered, "We have another problem. How can I sneak out of the apartment without Dad seeing me?"

CHAPTER

8

Heather was shocked awake by a loud gasp. "What's happened? What's the matter?"

Jamal clutched at the sheet. "It's . . . it's . . . I don't know how to tell you this, but you look like some kind of monster."

"Who, me? What are you talking about?"

Jamal pointed to the mirror. "You'd better have a look."

Heather rolled out of bed and padded to the dresser. When she saw her reflection, she shrieked, "Oh, no! I must have turned in my sleep! Now we'll have to start all over!"

"We'd better hurry." Jamal wiggled into her clothes. "Mom's picking me up in an hour."

Heather and Jamal shut themselves in the bedroom with the rubber gloves full of makeup. Jamal tilted a wicker chair and shoved it under the doorknob. Heather used the lotion for smashing down her arm hairs and to remove the smeared makeup.

"Do it just like Ashley," Heather said, dropping to the edge of the bed.

"No problem." Jamal carefully applied a layer of foundation. Baby-blue eye shadow and peach blush followed. A black pencil was used to draw a thin line under Heather's lower lashes.

They almost jumped out of their skins when Todd hammered on the bedroom door. "Hey, Jamal!" he shouted. "Your mom's here!"

"Already?" Heather whispered in a panic. "But we're not done!"

Jamal stuffed her pj's into her daypack. "Just finish under the lashes of your other eye," she said. "And add mascara."

"Okay," Heather said.

Jamal unhooked the chair and scurried off.

"Call me as soon as you get home from the party," she said over her shoulder.

Heather leaned into the mirror, armed with the black pencil. It was starting to get dull. Her line came out thicker than the one Jamal had drawn. A few extra coats of mascara would hide the difference. She looked at herself in the mirror and smiled. "Awesome."

But how am I going to leave the apartment without Dad seeing me? she suddenly wondered. *He thinks I bought a new outfit. Not a $9.99 makeover. He'll want a fashion show as soon as we eat breakfast.*

Why doesn't Dear Abby have an 800 number?

These were the thoughts that hammered her head while she flipped through hangers in her closet. TENNIS IS MY BAG and LIFE'S A VOLLEYBALL were her favorite sweatshirts. After trying on every top in her closet, she settled on a plain purple T-shirt. She tucked it into her jeans and slipped on the vest with ragged armholes.

Heather studied her digital clock. Maybe she

could leave Dad a note and sneak out before he got up. But the party didn't start for several hours. She pulled out a piece of her special HEATHER stationery and concentrated as if it were a school assignment.

"Dear Dad: I went to the pizza parlor early to help decorate for the party. I'll call you later. Don't worry." She chewed on the eraser. How should she sign it? "Your sneaky daughter" popped into her head. She shook away the notion and wrote, "Love, Heather."

"I knocked, but—"

Heather jumped.

"Heather?" Dad stood in the doorway, staring at her. "What in the world?"

Her throat was so dry she couldn't swallow, and she needed to swallow before she could talk. "Jamal and I were, ummm," she whispered, "just messing around."

"Well, wash up. And let's have breakfast," he said. "I'm making peanut-butter pancakes. Would you rather have smooth or crunchy?"

Heather squirmed. "Wash up?"

"You're not planning to go to the party like *that?*" Then it must have hit him. "Are you?"

"Every girl in my class wears mascara or *something,*" she snapped at him. "If Mom were here, she'd let me wear makeup. Especially to a party. Why do you treat me like such a baby?"

Heather brushed past him and stomped off to the bathroom. She didn't even slow down when he called after her, "Heather? Heather?"

So what if she hurt her dad's feelings? He deserved it. Now all her plans were ruined.

Heather scrubbed her face with a soapy washcloth until it was as red as a pickled beet. *What am I going to do now?*

The next hour was spent in her room sprawled on the floor, doodling a string of *O*s on a sheet of notebook paper—a connecting series of circles that reminded her of links in a bracelet. Using the eraser, she broke the chain in two. In the empty space she added a giant question mark.

What am I going to do?

She made a list of possible choices. Joining the Peace Corps was number one. Buying a mask was number twenty. In between were things like becoming a foreign-exchange student and joining the homeless.

Heather didn't open the door when her dad knocked. "I have a plate of pancakes," he said. "Please open the door, Heather. We have to talk about this."

"Go away," she kept saying.

Finally she heard him walk down the hall. There was only one thing to do—switch on the cordless phone and dial Justin's number.

"There's a serious illness in the family," she said, practicing her excuse while the phone rang on the other end. "We have to catch the next plane to Los Angeles."

The first part wasn't even a lie. She'd never felt so sick in her entire life.

Heather hung up when their answering machine clicked on. Justin's whole family was probably at the restaurant blowing up balloons and stringing crepe paper.

Justin will never speak to me again if I don't show up, she thought, throwing herself backward on the bed. *He'll never speak to me again if I do show up. Not after he finds out I lied about what I look like.*

She snatched the invitation off her nightstand. "Should I?" she asked, ripping it up. "Or shouldn't I?" The scraps of paper fell like flower petals. "Should I? Or shouldn't I?"

"Should I" won by a scrap. Heather rummaged through her drawers for her ski hat. She stuffed her hair into a scrunchy and pulled the hat down until it touched her eyebrows. It covered both her hair and her birthmark. Next she added sunglasses. No one would know if her hair was blond or if her eyes were green, and if she stood up straight she might pull off the tall part.

Heather picked up Justin's wrapped present and headed down the hall. Her dad looked up from the vacuum cleaner. Then he turned it off.

"Hi," he said.

"Hi," she said.

"Need a ride?" he asked.

Heather cleared her throat. "Okay." It wasn't too far to walk, but she didn't want to be late.

Heather followed her dad downstairs to the van. No one said anything for the first block. Her dad cleared his throat three times, then said, "I know it's difficult to talk to me about some things. But I wish you'd try."

Heather felt rotten for the remark she'd made about her mom. Not *every* girl in class wore makeup. How could she explain it so that her dad would understand? She decided to keep quiet.

"If I don't know the answer, maybe I can ask somebody," he went on. "Or maybe get a book from the library."

Heather exhaled loudly. She imagined her dad in the library, asking for a book on teenagers. He'd probably pronounce each syllable in *adolescence* as if it were a separate word.

The van eased to a stop in front of the pizza place. "Call me when the party's over," he said, "and I'll pick you up."

Her nod was weak. "Okay."

Heather stood on the curb and watched the van until it disappeared into traffic. Then she squatted next to a car, blinked in the side-view mirror, and applied a thick coat of Purple Passion lipstick.

She took a deep breath, as if getting ready to plunge into a pool, and dove for the front door. She jerked at the door handle and slipped inside.

"Heather?" someone said.

Heather squinted through her sunglasses. Even in the dim light the small brass stud in his left ear shined. *Jamal was right. He is a hunk. Just like the guy on our soap opera.* But she said, "Err . . . ummm . . . hi."

"What's with the sunglasses?" Justin said, lumbering forward. "And the ski hat? What're you, bald?"

Heather shuffled backward. "No . . . I'm . . . ," she muttered as heat crawled up her neck.

"Or is your hair green?" Justin grabbed for the hat. "Come on. I wanna see!"

CHAPTER
9

From the shadows behind Justin a shy voice murmured, "Heather?"

A shorter guy stepped around Justin. "I warned you about the sloth," he said. "He's extremely contagious."

Then it clicked. The voice. "Justin" wasn't Justin at all. He was Justin's stepbrother, the three-toed sloth.

Heather tried not to stare. But Justin's hair was the color of a basketball, and so were the frames of his glasses.

Heather sighed, relieved. She couldn't wait to tell Jamal that the guy dumping the trash wasn't

Justin. It was Sloth-Foot. Justin wasn't a tall, dark hunk. He was just a normal kid.

Jamal had been right. Justin had lied about the way he looked. Well, he hadn't lied, exactly. He just hadn't corrected her when she'd guessed he was tall with dark hair. But then she hadn't corrected him either.

"You didn't tell me your girlfriend was bald," Sloth-Foot said as he trotted to the tables at the back of the room.

Justin snapped, "She's not my *girl*friend."

"I tell my brother the same thing," Heather said quickly. "That you're a boy friend. Two words. Not *boy*friend, one word."

Justin nodded, then stared at the floor as if the sawdust contained top-secret information. Heather stared at it too. She roughed up a stain with the toe of her shoe and wondered if Justin was as self-conscious about his glasses as she was about her birthmark.

She also wondered why it was so hard to talk to him. On the phone they talked about all kinds of things. School activities and teachers. Friends and family. But now her mind was as blank as a freshly erased chalkboard.

The overhead speakers blasted an old Beach Boys song. "I wish they all could be California girls" bounced off the walls. Justin shifted his weight and studied the sawdust plastered on his shoes.

Heather fidgeted with her hat and flashed another sideways glance at Justin. *His eyes are brown,* she thought. *Not dirt-clod brown like mine. Or dark chocolate like Sloth-Foot's. Justin's eyes are the color of russet potatoes.*

Heather sucked in a deep breath. She wanted to tell Justin it was nice to meet him. And that she was glad he was a normal kid. But she didn't know how to arrange the words without sounding stupid. It was so much easier to talk to a telephone voice.

"How's your cold?" Justin asked.

"Cold?" Her nose started itching and she scratched it. "It's better."

"Sorry I didn't call you back," he said. "We

went to the airport to pick up my aunt and uncle."

Heather had forgotten about him calling. So much other stuff was happening. "It's okay."

"I saved us a booth," Justin said.

Heather gave a little nod and shuffled to the booth a few steps behind him. She accidentally bumped a high chair leaning against the wall. It wobbled as if it might fall down. The familiar blush spread up her neck. In seconds her cheeks would be brighter than a fire engine.

She slipped her sunglasses into her pocket, wondering, *Would Justin and I still be friends if we'd met at school? Would I have noticed him? Probably not. Would he have noticed me? Definitely not.*

Then her mind switched to Sloth-Foot. When she'd first seen him she'd thought he was a ten-plus. Of course, that was before she knew what a jerk he was. Now she thought he was a minus one hundred.

As they passed a row of video games lined up against the side wall, a woman in baggy sweats rushed over. It was Mrs. Steamer. "You must be Justin's new friend," she said. "Come in and meet the rest of the family."

Heather added her present to a table crowded with other wrapped boxes and glanced around the pizza parlor. There were enough people to fill a soccer stadium. At least that was how it seemed.

Heather flew around the room with Mrs. Steamer, stammering through a ton of nice-to-meet-yous. She shook hands with Justin's aunts and uncles and said hi to a bunch of cousins, including a guy in a T-shirt that read VISUALIZE WHIRLED PEAS.

Aunt Michelle's voice was somewhat high-pitched, but it didn't sound like screeching tires. Uncle George *did* tell a couple of dumb riddles. "What's black and white and red all over?" he asked.

Heather answered "A newspaper" in a polite voice, even though it was the first riddle she had learned in preschool.

"No," Uncle George said. "A skunk in a blender!"

88

Justin just tagged along behind them.

The whole family was looking at her with wide grins. *Are they laughing at my ski hat?* she wondered. *After all, it is ninety degrees outside.*

After the introductions, she excused herself and pushed into the rest room. In one sweeping motion she removed her ski hat and stuffed it into her back pocket. Then she wet her bangs and smashed them down on her forehead.

The whole operation took less than sixty seconds.

Heather returned to Justin, who was now parked in a corner booth. A *dark* corner booth. She slid across the seat on the other side of the table. The back of her jeans squeaked against the vinyl, making that embarrassing sound.

There was another strained silence.

Heather tried to think of something to say. Anything. But her only thoughts were, *I shouldn't have come to the party. We should've remained telephone friends.*

Neither one of them spoke for what seemed like a month. Then they both mumbled at the same time. Justin coughed into his hand and said, "What's taking the pizza?" Heather fingered her bangs and said, "This is a cool party."

When the pizza finally arrived, Justin set a slice on a napkin. He pushed it across the table. "It's your favorite kind," he muttered.

Heather smiled. "Thanks." But she was wondering, *Why is it so much easier to talk to you on the phone?*

Heather swallowed a sip of soda while peeking over the glass. Justin took a quick bite of pizza and chewed while holding a napkin over his mouth.

Heather also ate with her mouth closed. Nothing was worse than looking across the table at someone else's chewed-up food.

Mr. Steamer walked over. "Is everything okay?"

Heather said, "Uh-huh."

Justin just nodded.

Mr. Steamer smiled before he returned to the others. Everyone else gobbled pizza as fast as it was served. Wadded-up napkins and empty soft-drink pitchers topped every table.

Sloth-Foot strolled over next. "Why don't you open your presents?"

Justin ignored him.

Sloth-Foot sneezed. Something green and gooey flew out of his nose.

"Why don't you grow up!" Justin shot at him. Then he told Heather, "It's a peeled grape. I told you he was gross."

Heather rolled her eyes as if to say, "My brother's just as disgusting."

When the lights dimmed the room fell into darkness. A cake with candles appeared across the room. Rounds of "Happy Birthday" echoed around the flickering candles.

Heather joined in the singing. "Happy birthday to you . . ."

Justin suddenly shouted, "Get lost!"

"Happy birthday" caught in Heather's throat. "Huh?"

"I didn't even want you to come," he snapped.

Heather felt as if she'd been socked in the stomach. "Get lost?" she repeated under the next line of "Happy Birthday." If someone else had talked to her like that she would've been fighting mad. But coming from Justin—her only *boy* friend—it crushed her feelings.

Get lost! The words burned in her ears. She slipped silently from the booth and stumbled through the dark restaurant to the front door.

She didn't breathe until she was outside, where she fumbled for her sunglasses. But nothing could keep the tears from flooding her cheeks.

Her race home passed in a blur of mini-malls and traffic sounds.

Justin must've seen my artichoke when I took off my hat, she thought as she sprinted up the apartment stairs. *He just didn't have enough nerve to say anything until the lights went out. Dad was wrong. People do notice my birthmark. They do care what other people look like. At least some people do.*

Heather slammed into the apartment. Her stomach had that gnawing feeling she connected with tests. If she tried to eat one bite of food, she'd feel as if she'd eaten a seven-course meal. Full and bloated. Two bites and she'd barf what was left of last night's broiled chicken.

She hurried down the hall to her bedroom. The familiar furniture and posters should have been a comfort, but they weren't. She stared at the pile of dirty clothes on her closet floor and tossed in the wool cap.

There didn't seem to be anything else to do except collapse on the heap of clothes. She pulled the closet door shut and sobbed in the darkness. "I'm never coming out!" she cried, chomping on the sleeve of a sweatshirt. "And no one can make me!"

CHAPTER
10

"Heather?" Dad's voice floated through the closet door. "What's wrong?"

Justin's words came back in a flash. *"I didn't want you to come. Get lost."* She shook her head to erase the words.

"Did something happen at the party? Something with Justin?" Dad asked. "Come on, Heather. Let's talk about it."

Heather bit down even harder on her sweat-shirt sleeve. It tasted as bad as it smelled. Like week-old sweat. "I—I—I can't." She tried to steady the wobble in her voice. "I just can't."

Heather listened as her dad paced on the other

side of the closet. "Do you need some time alone? Is that it?"

Heather wanted to say, "Yes, Daddy. I need time. The rest of the century!"

"I'll be back in a little while," he said with a deep sigh. "Then we're going to talk."

Heather heard her bedroom door close. She slumped in the clothes pile. *Why didn't I leave my sunglasses on? And my ski hat? Why didn't I just stay home?*

A few minutes later, her bedroom door squeaked open again. "Hey, little sister," Todd said in a friendly voice. "Having a bad hair day?"

"Shut up," she snapped.

"I understand," he said lightly. "Sometimes life's as tough as beef jerky. Take that English test on Friday. I studied one whole hour and got a C-plus. Is that fair?"

Is that Todd the Hog? Trying to be nice? Or have aliens taken over his body?

"So I know what it's like when things don't work out," he rambled on.

Heather pressed her ear to the closet door. It sounded as if Todd was moving furniture. Her dresser, maybe. At least that was the direction of the sound.

"Testing," he said. Then the message on the answering machine filled the room. "This is the Reynolds residence. . . ."

"The answering machine is plugged in," Todd said. "Thought you'd want to hear any calls that might come in."

Heather couldn't believe it. Todd hadn't told Dad when he saw her with makeup. Was the trip to the mall only yesterday? Now he'd hooked up the answering machine in her room. Dad must have told him that something had happened at Justin's party.

Maybe he wasn't so bad after all—for an older brother.

Heather tugged on her bangs. What was she going to tell her dad when he came back? It would hurt too much to talk about Justin's party. Putting it into sentences, pausing at commas, stopping at periods, would be too much like being there.

Heather jumped when the phone rang. Jamal was probably calling to find out what happened at the party.

Ring. Ring. Ring.

The machine clicked on.

Justin's voice spilled out. "I'm sorry you left early. But I understand," he said. "Sloth-Foot is so-o-o-o gross. I would've split, too, except it was my party. I kept telling him to get lost. But he never listens to me."

Heather cracked the closet door. Had she heard him right? *"I kept telling him to get lost."*

Then he wasn't talking to me? He was talking to Sloth-Foot?

Heather crawled across the carpet. She slowly lifted the phone and said, "Uh—hi."

"Hi. It's Justin."

Heather chewed her lip, and repeated, "Uh—hi. Were you really talking to Sloth-Foot?"

"Well, yeah," Justin said. "Who else?"

"I thought you were talking to me," she said quietly. "That's why I left."

"You? Heck no." He sounded surprised. "Sloth-Foot sneaked up on me when the lights were off. I knew he was planning something gross, so I told him to get lost," Justin said. "Guess that's why you were so quiet, huh? Because Sloth-Foot was such a jerk when you first got there. Plus his trick with the peeled grape."

Heather let herself smile. "I thought *you* were quiet."

"Me? Quiet?" Then he said, "Yeah, well . . . I didn't know what to say. It was a lot different than talking on the phone."

"Now *that's* weird," she said. "I felt the same way."

"Really?"

"Yeah." Heather twisted the telephone cord around her finger. "Guess I was worried that you wouldn't like me after we met. Funny, huh? When we started being friends on the phone I never thought about that stuff. But then I lied about what I look like . . . I don't even know why. It was dumb."

"I did the same thing," he added in a low voice. "And you're right. It was stupid."

Heather continued, "Sometimes when I write in my diary I don't think about it. The words just seem to pour out of my pen. That's how I feel when we're on the phone. The words just pour out."

"Yeah," he agreed. "When we were in the booth I kept trying to think of something to say. But my mind was totally blank."

Heather laughed. "Me too!"

"Besides, I didn't want to talk too much." He paused a moment before saying, "I didn't want you to see my braces."

"Do you have braces?"

"Just on top," he said. "Didn't you see them?"

"No, I didn't. Anyway, braces are no big deal. Most kids get them sooner or later. I'll be getting them, too. It's different than having a humongous birthmark."

"Do you have a birthmark?"

Heather blinked, wide-eyed. "Don't tell me you didn't see it?"

"Huh-uh."

Heather paused and squinted through her bangs. "It's on my forehead. And it's shaped like an artichoke."

"I love artichokes."

Heather heard herself laugh. "Maybe I should be thankful it's not shaped like a broccoli spear."

"Yeah, broccoli is gross," he said. "Our kitchen smells like burning rubber when Mom cooks broccoli."

Heather sighed. "Guess we all have stuff about ourselves we don't like."

Did those words really come out of her mouth? She couldn't believe it. Both Dad and Jamal had been right. Most people didn't notice her artichoke. Those who did notice didn't care. Just like she didn't care about Justin's braces.

"Since we figured out why it was hard to talk to each other," Justin said, "do you think we should try it again? Maybe meet for a soda some-time?"

"What do you think?" Heather asked.

They both paused for a moment, then blurted, "Not!" and laughed.

Heather caught her breath. "At least not for a while. Besides, why should we?" she added. "What would we talk about over a soda that we can't talk about on the phone?"

"Judging from the party," Justin put in, "not much."

They laughed again.

Heather turned toward the gentle tap on her door. "Can I call you later?" she said to Justin. "I have to talk to my dad."

"Sure," he said. "And thanks for the CD. Watermelon Seed is too cool. 'Together We Jam' is my favorite song."

"See ya."

"Bye."

Heather hung up and glanced at herself in the mirror. Her eyes were swollen and as puffy as unbaked biscuits. They felt as if they were filled with coarse salt.

She swiveled toward the door. "Come in."

Dad strolled wearily into the room. He looked as exhausted as she felt. "Are you okay?"

Heather nodded.

He lowered himself onto the edge of her bed. "Feel like talking?"

Heather plucked a tissue from the box on her dresser. She blew her nose, then dropped down next to her dad on the bed. Before she knew it, she'd told him everything that had happened. "I thought Justin didn't like me . . . that he was sorry I was there. . . ." She swallowed a lump in her throat that felt like an ice cube. "I even thought he wanted me to leave the party."

Dad wrapped his arm around her shoulder. "Why would you think something like that?"

"When the lights were turned down and everyone was singing 'Happy Birthday'—well, Justin shouted, 'Get lost!' I thought he was talking to me. But he was really talking to his stepbrother, Sloth-Foot."

Dad squeezed her shoulder. "I guess I forgot how hard it is to be your age."

Heather blurted out the rest of the story before she lost her nerve. "I didn't use the credit slip to buy a new outfit," she admitted between sniffles. "I bought a makeover at the department store. So Justin would like me."

"Oh, Heather," her dad said with a low sigh. "It seems like just last week that you were my little girl. Now look at you. You're almost a teenager. Guess I haven't been paying attention to how quickly you're growing up."

"It isn't you, Daddy. It's my dumb birthmark," she said. "But you were right. It isn't important. At least not as important as I thought it was. I might even stop trying to cover it with makeup."

Dad's eyebrows arched on the word *makeup*.

Heather tossed the wadded tissue into the wastebasket. "Mom wouldn't have let me wear makeup to the party. I'm sorry I said that."

Dad gathered her into a warm hug. "It's okay, Heather. *Everything* is okay." Then he added,

"You and Justin have become real friends. That kind of relationship goes a lot deeper than a layer of makeup."

Heather let her head rest on his shoulder. She didn't even care that he'd thrown in a small lecture. "I know that now," she said with a sniffle. "I love you, Daddy."

"I love you, too," he said. "Remember, you're not alone, Heather. I'm here anytime you need to talk. It doesn't matter what it's about. Don't forget that, okay?"

Heather knew she could always count on her dad. But hearing him say it out loud reassured her. "I won't forget," she said.

They exchanged another squeeze before Dad stood up. "How about a couple of good old American hamburgers?" he asked.

Heather was suddenly starving. "With tons of ketchup!"

"I'll toast the buns," he said, "if you'll slice the dill pickles."

"It's a deal."

Heather grabbed the cordless phone as soon as her dad strolled off toward the kitchen. In an instant she'd punched in Jamal's number. "You won't believe what happened at Justin's party!" she said, heading down the hall.